Kristie's Excellent A

The Deep Blue Sea

by Geri McNeely Schultz

with Illustrations by Vince Bertolami

Kristie's Excellent Adventures:
The Deep Blue Sea
Written by Geri McNeely Schultz

Cover Illustrations by Vince Bertolami

Windy City Publishers
2118 Plum Grove Road #349
Rolling Meadows, IL 60008
www.windycitypublishers.com

Published in the United States of America

ISBN:
978-1-941478-14-1

Library of Congress Control Number:
2015941640

Chicago

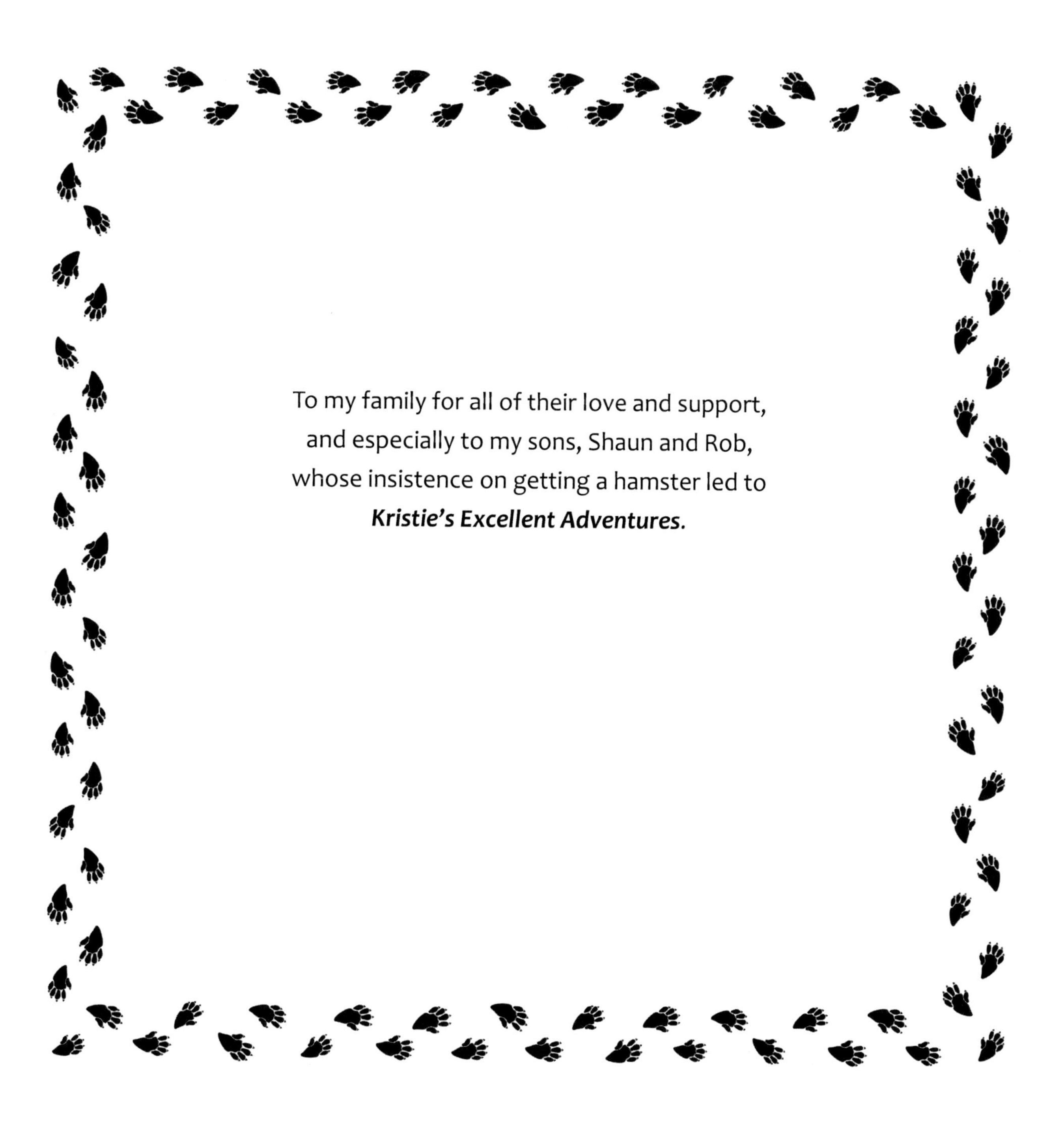

To my family for all of their love and support,
and especially to my sons, Shaun and Rob,
whose insistence on getting a hamster led to
Kristie's Excellent Adventures.

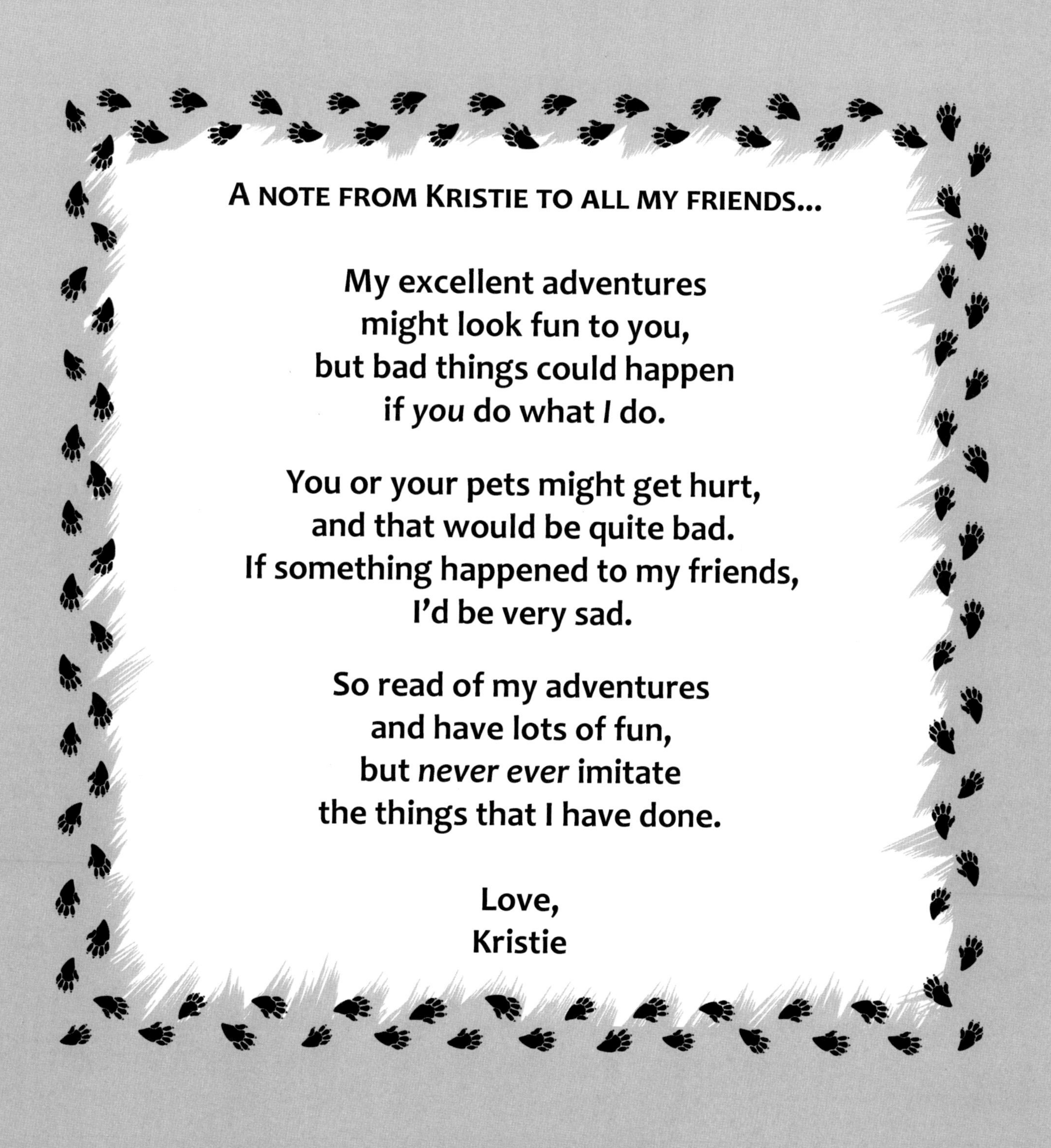

A NOTE FROM KRISTIE TO ALL MY FRIENDS...

My excellent adventures
might look fun to you,
but bad things could happen
if *you* do what *I* do.

You or your pets might get hurt,
and that would be quite bad.
If something happened to my friends,
I'd be very sad.

So read of my adventures
and have lots of fun,
but *never ever* imitate
the things that I have done.

Love,
Kristie

Kristie woke one morning and thought
I want to play.
What excellent adventure
can I have today?

She popped out of her hamster cage
up in the laundry room,

leaped off the shelf onto the floor
and landed with a boom!

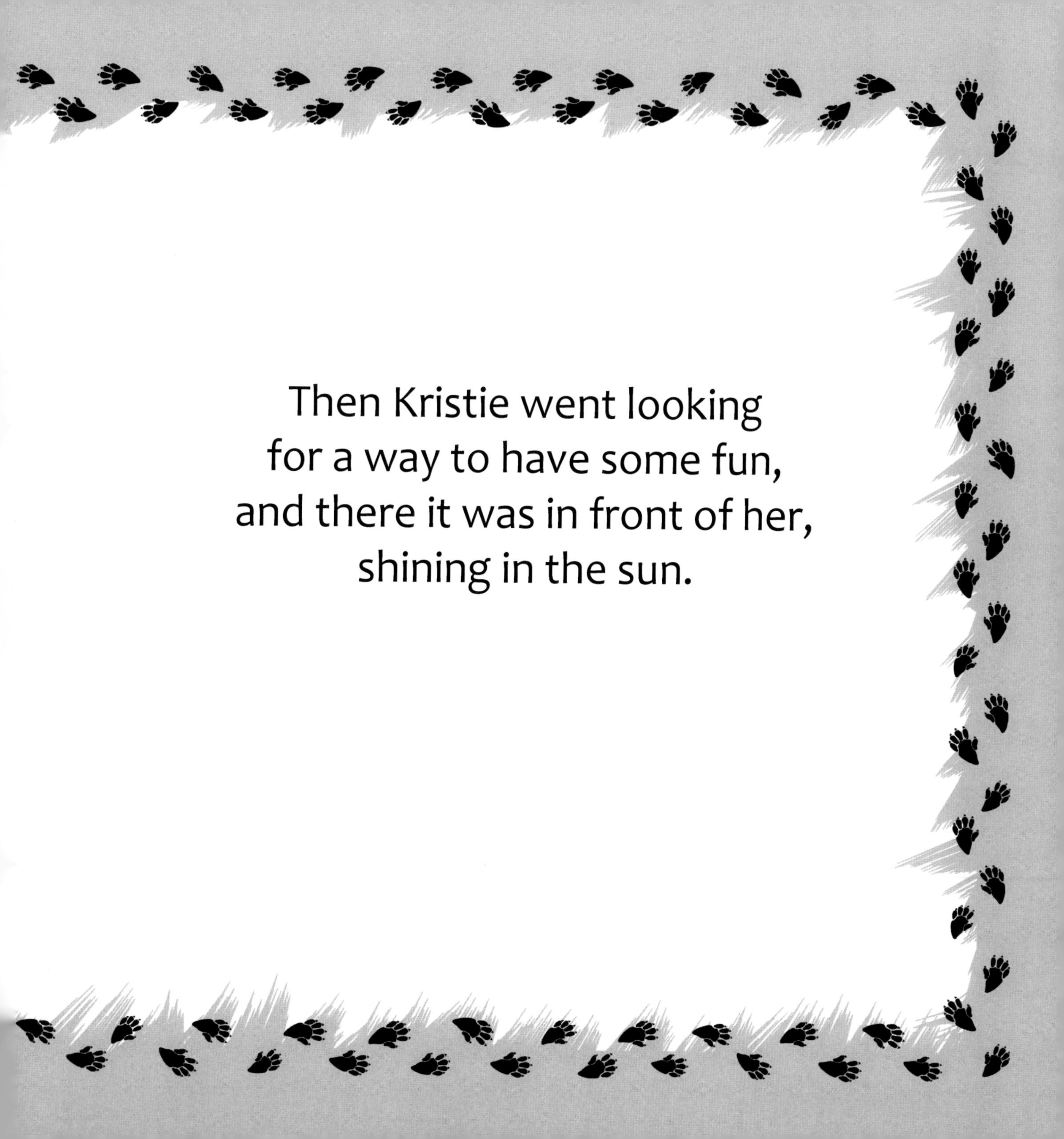

Then Kristie went looking
for a way to have some fun,
and there it was in front of her,
shining in the sun.

A big clear box of water
with brightly colored things.

As Kristie scampered closer,
some looked like they had wings.

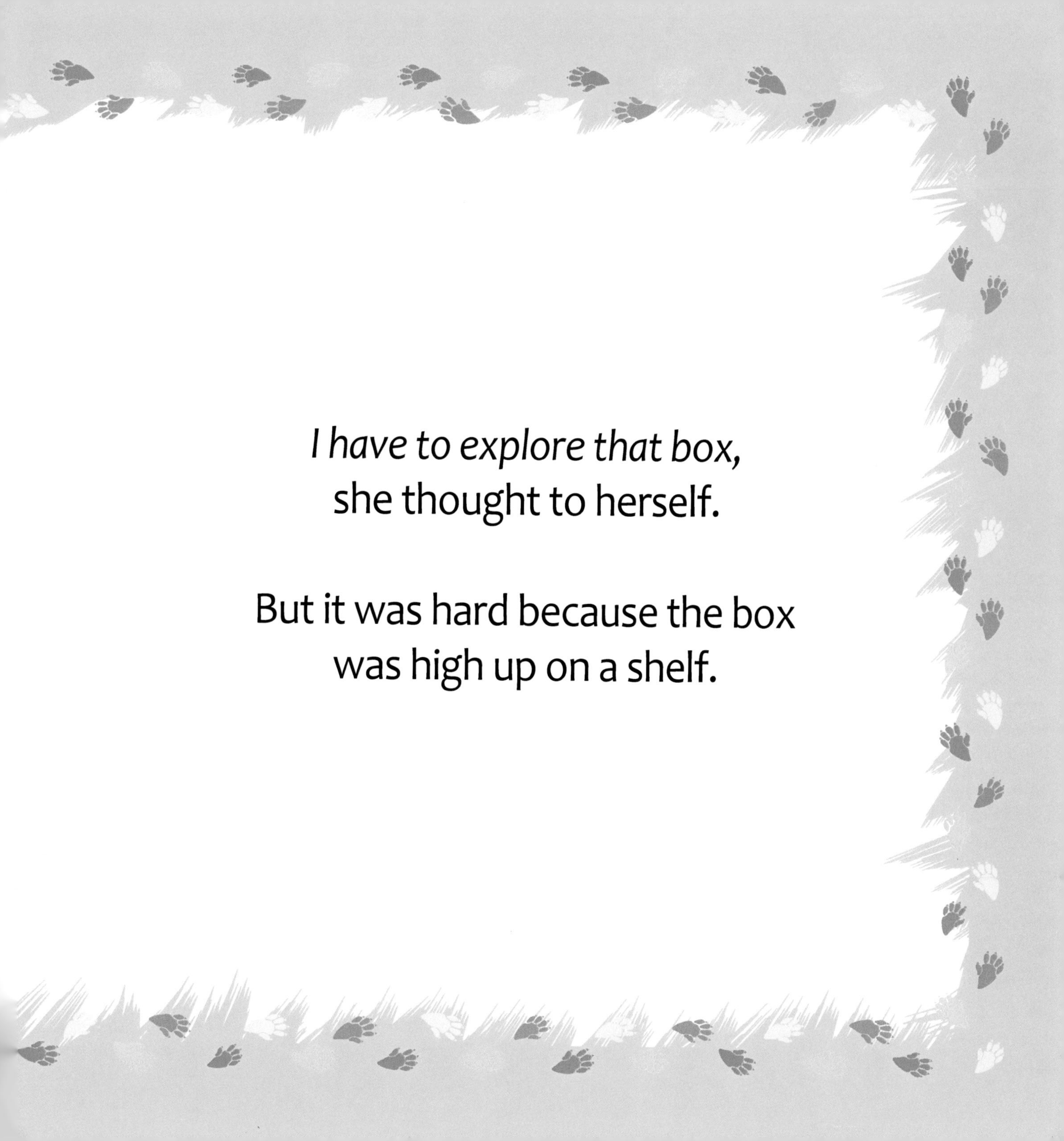

I have to explore that box,
she thought to herself.

But it was hard because the box
was high up on a shelf.

She scampered closer to the box,
and climbed up on a chair,
then bounced onto the cushion
and flew up in the air.

But oops… she flew too high and far
and certainly too fast.

And, before she knew it,
she landed with a splash!

As Kristie looked around her,
her eyes popped open wide.

She could not believe the things
this clear box had inside.

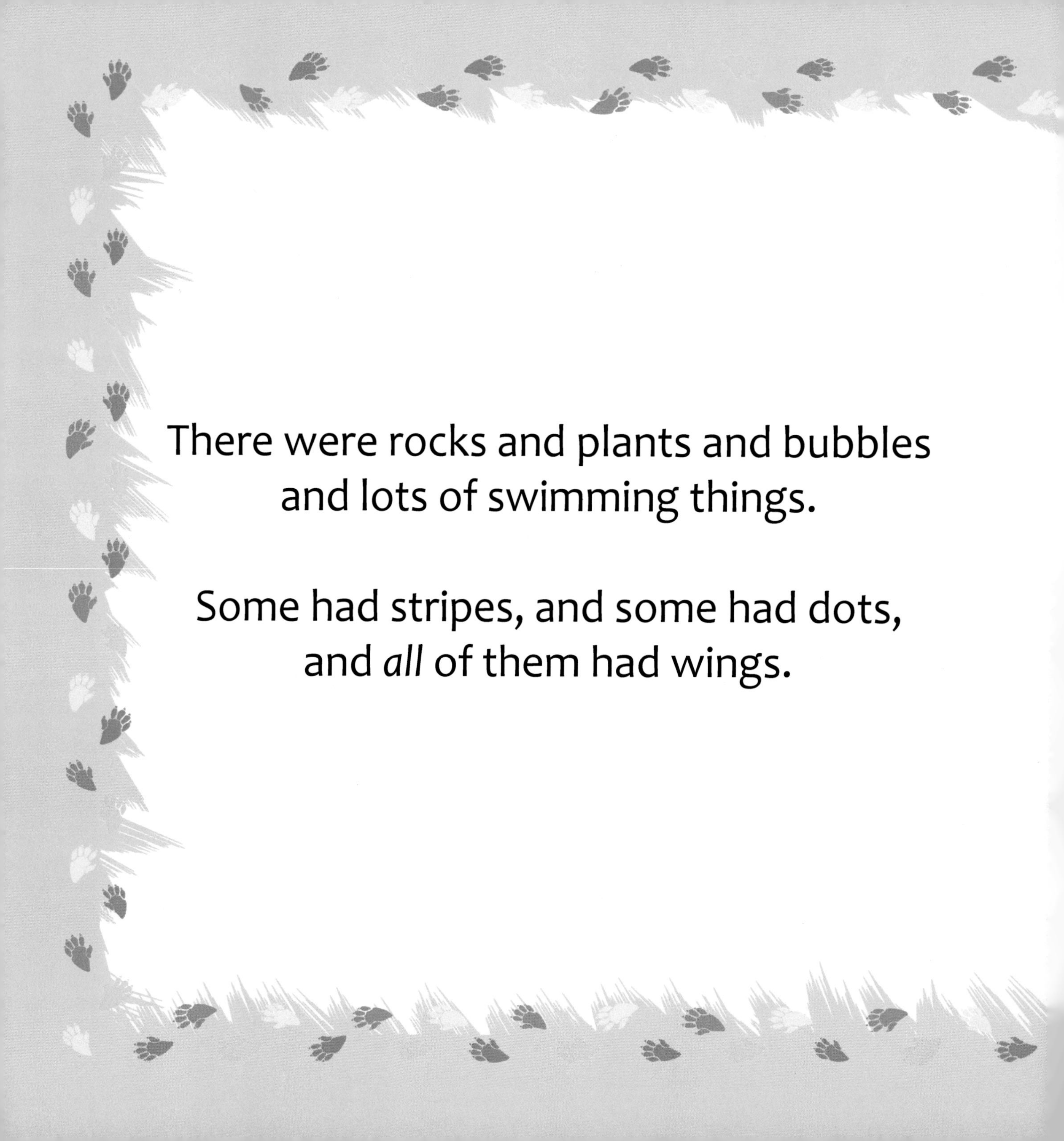

There were rocks and plants and bubbles
and lots of swimming things.

Some had stripes, and some had dots,
and *all* of them had wings.

Some were big and yellow,
and some were red and small.

Some were green, and some were blue,
and Kristie liked them all.

Kristie met a starfish.
Then she met a snail.

Then she met a turtle
with a tiny tail.

Then Kristie saw something strange
that looked like a spaceman.

It talked to her in bubbles…
“Hi! I’m diver Dan.”

Hi

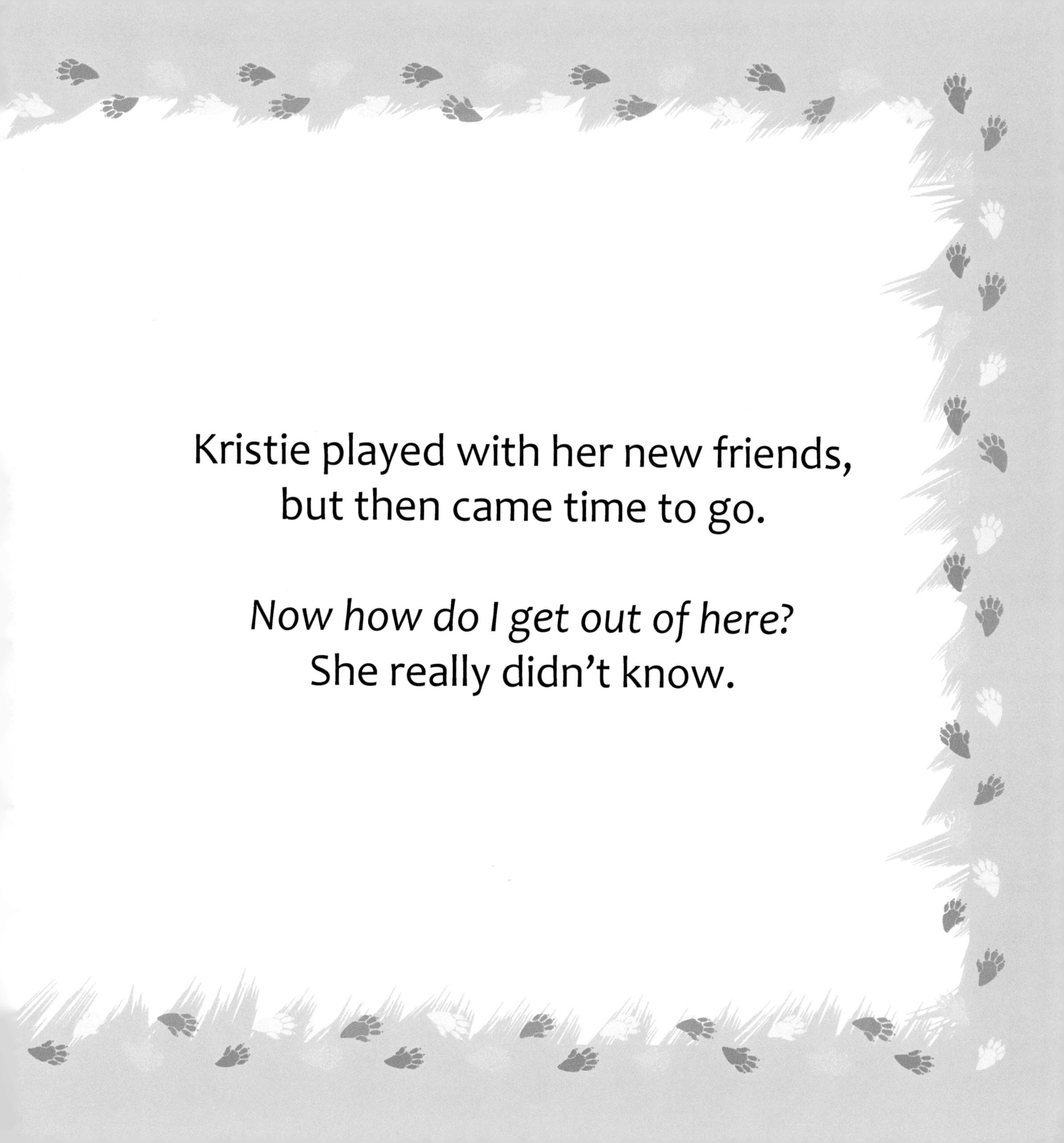

Kristie played with her new friends,
but then came time to go.

Now how do I get out of here?
She really didn't know.

Kristie was a little scared,
and she began to pout,
but diver Dan raised her up,
and Mommy scooped her out.

As Mommy put her back into her cage,
she heard her say,

"That's enough adventure,
Little Kristie, for one day."

Sleepy little Kristie
snuggled in her cozy bed,
with memories of her excellent
adventure in her head.

She closed her eyes and smiled,
remembering the fun,
and thought about the
excellent adventures still to come.

Made in the USA
Las Vegas, NV
12 November 2021

34277740R00024